MAID FOR TWO
BY
STACY-DEANNE
VENUS RAY

Copyright © 2022 Stacy-Deanne

ALL RIGHTS RESERVED: The unauthorized reproduction or distribution of this copyrighted work is illegal. Criminal copyright infringement is investigated by the FBI and is punishable by up to 5 years in federal prison and a fine of $250,000.

All characters and events in this book are fictitious. Any resemblance to actual persons living or dead is strictly coincidental.

Readers: Thanks so much for choosing my book! I would be very appreciative if you would leave reviews when you are done. Much love!

Email: stacydeanne1@aol.com

Website: Stacy's Website [1]

1.　https://www.stacy-deanne.com/

Facebook: Stacy's Facebook Profile[2]
Twitter: Stacy's Twitter[3]

To receive book announcements subscribe to Stacy's mailing list: Mailing List[4]

2.	https://www.facebook.com/stacy.deanne.5

3.	https://twitter.com/stacydeanne

4.	https://stacybooks.eo.page/cjjy6

NOTE TO READERS:

Thanks for picking up this book. The Sex in the Wild West Series is a historical interracial erotic short story series featuring black women and white men couples. Each book stands alone. This means that you don't have to read them in any specific order! If you enjoy this story then make sure to check the webpage dedicated to the series. On this page you will see the books released as well as books that are upcoming so you can preorder. You can also keep up with the series on its Amazon series page under Stacy-Deanne or Venus Ray.

KEEP UP WITH THE SEX IN THE WILD WEST SERIES HERE:

CLICK HERE[1]

IMPORTANT: You can also sign up for the *Sex in the Wild West Series* mailing list. You will get an email whenever a new book releases! Note, if you are a subscriber to Stacy's regular mailing list then you still need to sign up for this one if you want information on this series. Stacy will not be sending mailings about this series to her existing list since these books are erotica.

    Sign up here: https://stacybooks.eo.page/rd687
    Enjoy!

---

1. **https://www.stacy-deanne.com/sexwildwest.html**

CHAPTER ONE

Wilkerson, Montana 1895

Twenty-one-year-old Clara had no reason to complain. She was an uneducated Negro who had the lucky opportunity of being the maid to one of the most prestigious families in Wilkerson, Montana.

As she dusted around the Crawford parlor, full of chiseled furniture and lavish portraits, she thought of how lucky she was to have been born after 1865. Being a Negro maid in the lily-white Wilkerson could be difficult, but nothing compared to the outrage, humiliation, and degradation her ancestors felt during slavery every day of their lives.

No. Nothing compared to being whipped and treated like an animal. And though some folks in Wilkerson would prefer her kind didn't exist, they accepted them and, Negroes found different opportunities. Many migrated from the South after the Emancipation Proclamation because people here were more... tolerable. Yet, Clara's golden opportunity didn't keep her from being extremely bored.

She walked around all day, doing chores with the other Negro housekeeper, Junie. Sure, she had more than enough to keep her physically busy, but not to occupy her mind. Maybe it was the lack of a formal education that accounted for her great imagination. If she'd gone to school and learned something other than cleaning, she might not be wishing she were somewhere else every single day. She could further appreciate being able to live in a three-floor palace worth more money than the town itself.

The Crawfords were the richest family this side of Montana. People often came to them instead of the local bank to borrow. Wilkerson was a tiny speck of nothing and poor people either had dreams or heartache. But the boredom? Dear Lord. It was like a disease. It creeped in at the

most surprising time.

Clara didn't *deserve* a better life. A more fulfilling life, but she wanted it. She desired to travel. She wanted to see the world and step out of her comfort zone. Wanted to sample new people, new worlds, and cultures. Most of all, she wanted to be taken. Oh, yes. Being a virgin made her sick.

Only a dick or two could cure this hunger inside of her. Seeing how she wasn't getting out of this

town anytime soon, the only choice she had was to get her craving from sex. But from who?

She found Mr. Crawford utterly disgusting. A fat, yellow-toothed man with a limp and a bad attitude. He sweat so much it could feel a tub. His only good point was that he had plenty of money and knew how to keep making it. It had to be the only reason his wife, Mistress Bethany, who wasn't but a few years older than Clara herself, put up with him. Why else would a plump, delicious, doe-eyed blonde who could have any man in town want this tub of lard?

Clara wanted riches and the life Mr. Crawford could give, but she sure as hell didn't want *him*.

Junie fluttered into the room, flustered as always. Only a few years older than Clara, she'd tucked her dreams away years ago and though she was the only friend Clara had, Clara would die before she ended up like Junie, just surviving but not living.

"The cook just finished the peach cobbler... ooh." Junie clasped her hands, her chunky hips jiggling as she shook. "She wants us to taste it first. Don't you want some?"

"Pie?" Clara slumped into the chair made of fine upholstery and hand-carved wood. "Is a man in it?"

"What?" Junie whipped around and closed the double doors for privacy. "What are you talking about now, girl? That fantasy of yours? Hmph. Might as well knock it out of your head because this life right here... it's the best you gonna get."

"What's the point of dreaming if nothing comes of it?" Clara dropped the dust rag on the floor beside her feet. "I love you, Junie, but I don't wanna end up like you or the older maids who just work in the same household for years and years. I wanna experience life." Clara wiggled, her large bosom bouncing. "I wanna see all life offers without a care in the world!"

"You a Negro, girl." Junie grimaced. "Dreamin' is all you can do because nothing else gonna happen. You are lucky to be here in a beautiful home with your own room and taken care of. You wanna be out *there*?" She pointed to the double-hung window. "You been spoiled, Clara. You started working here when you was fourteen so you never had to fight out there. In here, you can forget you just a Negro because you're safe. But trust me..." Junie walked to the window, the hem of her cotton dress brushing against her black, lace-up boots. "You don't wanna be out *there*. I beg you to stop dreaming because it's just gonna make you feel worse."

Clara stood and stuck her chin in the air. "Why can't I get the life I want? That's the difference between you and me, Junie. I don't think being Negro should mean I can't be happy!"

Junie did a belly-laugh. "That's that spoiled brat talkin'. You wouldn't last a day if you weren't working here. You don't know how good you have it and I'm tired of you complaining, girl!"

The doors slid open and Mistress Bethany Crawford flounced inside, her sky-blue dress hugging her violin-shape from the bodice to the laces of her boots. "What is going on in here?" She stuck her little pointy chin in the air, waving her new fan in front of her face. "I declare. You two are always fussing. I'm expecting Mrs. Bronwell for tea shortly. I surely hope you get yourselves together by then."

"Mistress Bethany, I'm so sorry!" Junie floated over to her, kissing up as usual. "Forgive us. I was just telling Clara how lucky we both are to be in your home and working for such a lovely family."

"That you are." Clara nodded, her yellow hair piled onto her head in spirals and held together with fancy hairpins outlined in pearls. "We're all lucky to be here, even me. Oh." She strolled around all dramatic as usual, leaning on the piano Clara had just dusted. "The day Mr. Crawford proposed was the best day of my life. As you both know, I wasn't accustomed to such wealth. Daddy worked hard to provide for Momma, me and my eight brothers and sisters but never did I dream I'd be a Crawford.." Her green eyes danced as she looked across the room. "I'd do anything not to mess that up and I ain't even a Negra!"

"Yes, ma'am." Junie nodded. "You appreciate what you have. That's what Clara needs to do. It's so much harder out there and I don't think she understands that."

Bethany squinted at Clara. "Well, she'd better if she wants to keep working here. Mr. Crawford wouldn't be none too happy to realize one of his maids wished she was somewhere else."

"Oh, no." Clara curtsied. "I am so grateful for all that's been awarded to me. Believe me, I know how lucky I am, Mistress."

"Then show me your appreciation." Bethany strutted to Clara and stuck her polished boot out. "Kiss my boot and I won't utter a word of this to Mr. Crawford."

Clara looked at Junie.

"Mistress Bethany," Junie said. "Please, can we just forget this? We both sorry if we caused any hurt feelings."

"I believe *you*, Junie." Bethany batted her long lashes, glaring at Clara. "But Clara needs to

prove it. Don't stand there, girl." Bethany gestured to Clara with her fan. "Get down on your knees and show me how much you appreciate the life you've been awarded."

Clara fidgeted. It wasn't that Mistress Bethany hadn't humiliated her before but Bethany wasn't some revered person. Far from it. Most in town couldn't stand her and thought she was a floosy after Mr. Crawford's money. She didn't come from the level of wealth he did, so it enraged Clara that Bethany thought *she* had the right to treat her like an animal.

But she had that right. For she was a pretty, young, blonde, rich white woman and Clara was well... just the maid.

"On your knees, girl." Bethany smirked. "Now. And keep your lips there until I say otherwise."

"Mistress please," Junie said. "You don't have to do this—"

"Hush up now or I'll make her lick the *horse's* shoe! On your knees, Clara. I won't say it again."

Holding her breath, Clara knelt. She closed her eyes, her nose tickling from the smell of leather and fresh polish.

"That's it. Kiss it." Bethany wiggled her foot. "Right on the tip."

Clara might've been mistaken, but with the way Mistress Bethany's eyes lit up and the raunchy smirk on her face, she got the feeling this might've turned her on. Whatever the case, Clara ached to get this moment over with. She took a deep breath and puckered her lips.

"That's it," Bethany whispered. "Go on. Kiss my boot."

Clara inched her mouth closer, little by little.

A ruckus broke out in the front hall and Clara and Bethany jumped back.

"What in the world?" Bethany gasped, her white bosom spilling from her V-neck gown.

Clara heard grumbling and men talking amongst themselves while they tossed over furniture, threw porcelain ornaments and broke glass.

"Robbers!" Bethany gasped. "Oh, Junie, help me!"

The two women grabbed the large round table on opposite sides and attempted to slide it to the doors to block the men from entering, but the doors flew open and two huge, white men wearing all-black and in masks charged inside.

"Don't anyone move!" The dark-haired one said, waving his pistol. "We want the goods."

"We warning you." The blond, curly-haired man yelled. "One move or you try anything and we'll blow you to smithereens."

"How *dare* you?" Bethany stood beside Junie, shaking, with her arms up. "I'm Bethany Crawford, the lady of this house! You know who my husband is?"

"Course we do, you dumb harlot," the black-haired one, who was obviously the leader, snarled. "Why the hell you think we're here? Your jewelry. Throw it into this bag, now!" He held the bag out.

The way Bethany stood there as if her entire world was over, Clara almost felt sorry for her.

Almost.

"Hurry!" Black Hair snatched the pearl necklace off Bethany's neck. "The bracelet and the earrings. Get 'em off!"

While Bethany and Junie stood there, trembling like two newborn birds, Clara never felt so alive. Her heart raced and her knees knocked. Sure, Junie and Bethany shivered as well, but not for the same reasons. Theirs was out of terror while Clara's was from *excitement*.

The blond one tossed his fiery-brown gaze toward Clara and ran his tongue slowly across his dry lips. "What do we have here?" He stomped toward her in leather boots as black as the rest of his clothes. "You're a delicious-looking thing, aren't you?" He addressed the leader, "Look at what we got here."

"Ah." Black Hair gazed upon Clara and it was as if he'd forgotten about the jewelry. He licked his lips, chest heaving. "Looks like we found the most valuable thing of all."

Clara smirked, but then wiped it away when she remembered she was supposed to be scared.

"Please, sir," Junie said. "Don't hurt her."

"I don't care what you do with the varmint," Bethany rattled off. "You want her, you can take her. Just leave my jewels."

Black Hair raised his elbow and slammed it into Bethany's face, drawing blood and knocking her into the piano.

"Miss Bethany!" Junie helped her up.

"Oh!" Bethany hollered, holding her nose. "My nose. You animal!"

It was hard as hell for Clara not to just bust out laughing.

"We're taking her *and* the jewels." Blond rubbed his crotch and Clara noticed the lumpy

budge.

The only penis she'd seen was her little brother's when their momma bathed him as a baby. Hadn't seen one since and certainly not one from a white man.

Clara's breathing grew more rapid as she imagined all the things she wanted to do with him. With the both of them. He wouldn't need his hand anymore.

"You heard him, girl?" Black Hair ran his tongue across his gleaming teeth. "We taking you with us and you gonna do as we say. You understand?"

"No!" Junie dropped to her knees, begging for Clara's safety like she was her mother. "Please, don't take her. She done nothing!"

Black Hair raised his pistol to her. "You wanna be hit too?"

Junie crawled back over to Bethany and the women held each other, sobbing.

The robbers took Clara by each arm and dragged her outside to their carriage. They didn't *have* to drag her, but if it excited them for her to play the victim, she'd play it in spades.

CHAPTER TWO

Yipping and hollering, the men tossed Clara into the carriage and they all galloped off.

As she sat crammed in between them, her breasts bouncing and her tight mound aching for their touch, she got a feeling this was just the beginning. Perhaps her dream life awaited her and it started with these two gun-toting bucks who'd taken her against her will. Or at least they thought they had.

It was almost impossible to sit between them, smelling the musk radiating from their sweaty shirts and Clara not screech out in delight. But she had to keep the ruse going. She wouldn't ruin this for the world.

Every time Black Hair yanked those reins, steering the horses through the mountainous, sunny valley, more pressure and fullness built inside her pussy. So tender. Aching for the desperation to be touched. A pain that only their mouths, tongues and organs could take away.

"Whoa." Blond rocked beside her as the horses struggled up a rocky surface. "Are you afraid?" She could only see half his face, but a blind man could see how handsome he was. Square jaws. Golden stubbly lips made for sucking. Both men were desirable in different ways.

Black Hair took charge. No-holds-barred. Made his own rules. The man your momma warned you about but that you couldn't stay away from. A man who'd probably conquered more than his fair share of maidenheads.

Then Blond. Just as rough around the edges, but more mysterious. He wasn't as predictable as Black Hair. Wasn't in-your-face. The silent type until he had to scream, perhaps. Clara enjoyed his personality most of all. With Black Hair, you knew what you were getting at first glance. But with Blond, well, he kept you guessing and there was nothing more exciting than that.

"Where are we going?" she'd dared asked. Not that she really cared, but she hoped the trip wouldn't take much longer. She was so wet she was afraid she'd soil the carriage.

"A place where we can be alone." Black Hair's lips formed a devilish smirk. "Where no one can hear you moaning or screaming." He cackled. "Penny for your thoughts."

She continued to play the part. "I beg you, sir, to take mercy on me."

"Oh, we're gonna take you all right." Blond laughed. "And you'll be begging for mercy soon enough."

She snickered to herself. They didn't know the trouble they'd just stirred up. The amounts

of sexual deviancy she was about to release on this clueless, unsuspecting twosome. They talked the talk, but did they walk the walk? Who would win this game? Would they be able to tame her desire that she was so desperate to unleash?

"Ya!" Black Hair pulled the reins, stopping the carriage with a quick jolt. The horses stood there looking around and suddenly Clara got uncomfortable. She didn't want the horses watching.

"Please, sirs." She faked a whimper. "Not in front of the horses."

They looked at each other and laughed.

"You better hope we don't fuck you *on* the horses," Blond said, hopping out of the carriage. "My lady?" He held out his gloved hands, all gentleman like, and Clara took them and exited the carriage.

Black Hair hopped out afterwards and snatched Clara's arm without warning. They pulled her toward the rocks, her boots dragging on dirt and gravel.

"Please, I beg you!" She tried to make herself cry, but couldn't. "Is there anything I can do to stop this?"

"No," Black Hair said. "There's nothing you can do to stop this."

The men let her go and formed a fence in front of her.

"Nothing I can do to stop this, you say?" Clara looked back and forth at them, her temperature rising. "Well... *good.*"

Black Hair squinted underneath his mask.

Blond gaped and looked at his partner to see his expression.

"What are you waiting for?" Clara stepped out of her plain, white dress and snatched the maid's bonnet off her head.

The men watched her wide-eyed as she stood before them in her boots and short-sleeve chemise, the wind blowing the light material across her breasts.

Seeing how the men were just standing there, she was glad to get things moving. She dropped to her knees and unbuttoned Blond's pants. His breathing came out in hesitant pants as she lifted his thick meat and stroked it.

"Oh." He closed his eyes.

Black Hair grimaced. Perhaps jealous she'd picked Blond first, but he didn't have to worry, Clara would get to him soon enough.

"Oh..." Blond thrust his sweaty shaft back and forth inside her mouth.

Clara had never felt so powerful. Now she understood why Mr. Crawford spent so much time with the painted ladies down at the saloon. Sex wasn't just about the physical, it was about all the emotions it stirred up and with this delicious, thick dick in her mouth, everything became clear. Yes, Clara was on her way to a new world. A new life and she wasn't ever going back.

"Come here!" Black Hair pulled her up, her mouth still open from sucking. Huffing and puffing, he snatched his pants down and shoved his rock hard cock into her mouth. "Oh. Yes." Squeezing her head tightly, he moved it back and forth while she licked all around his shaft. "You're a virgin? Huh?"

Clara let his dick go with a smack. "Not for long."

He grinned as he plunged his dick so far into her mouth she gagged and gurgled, but it just made her feel more powerful to bring him to the depths of desire.

Blond dropped to his knees in behind her and hiked up her dress. He massaged her buttocks, then placed tender kisses where his hands used to be.

Clara sucked Black Hair while Blond spread her cheeks and rubbed his cock against her slit.

Blond was gentler than she imagined he would be. If this were a normal ravishing, he'd have just shoved it in her. And she was so glad he hadn't. Yes, she'd hungered for this moment, but she wanted them all to enjoy it unselfishly. Each giving pleasure and equally receiving it.

And that's exactly what happened. While Black Hair enjoyed her mouth, she sank back onto Blond's dick and flinched at the piercing pain as he entered her. But within seconds, her need outweighed any displeasure and her pussy widened, welcoming the extent of his girth.

"Yes, yes." Blond held her by her waist, bringing her back on his cock as Black Hair pumped her mouth until the corners of it were sore.

"I..." Black Hair closed his eyes, his mask still in place, though she wished she could see his face. "Oh, she's making me come. She's making me come! Ah." Surprisingly, like a gentleman, he pulled out before his seed hit her mouth.

Blond kept going as if in another world. Mumbling and moaning, his fingers digging into her skin. "This Negro pussy is good. Oh... God. It's heaven."

Licking her lips, Clara looked at him over her shoulder and again became even more turned

on at how much pleasure she'd brought both men already. "Don't stop," she whispered. "Harder.

Deeper."

Sweat cascaded from underneath Black Hair's mask as he pulled his pants down to his ankles and stroked himself. His slick sweat covering his gloves within seconds.

"That's it." Black Hair sucked his lips. "Keep fucking her. Is she tight? Is her cunt tight?"

"Oh, yes." Blond lifted her up, pounding harder. "Feels so good on my cock. Ah." He came, but unlike Black Hair, he didn't pull out. He flooded right inside of Clara and she wouldn't have had it any other way.

"This is my fantasy." She turned around on all fours and took Blond into her mouth. "Suck on me," she ordered Black Hair. "Please."

He dropped to his knees behind her, spread her cheeks and started licking.

"Ooh." She jerked from spasms. She felt as though her body were closing in on her. Every breath crushed her organs while the lingering smell of their sweat and body odor just heightened her desire more.

If she'd known it would feel this good, she'd have lost her virginity a long time ago. But it couldn't have been to just anyone. Or any two. It had to be these men. This was fate and her robbers had engraved themselves into her heart with each stroke and kiss.

Did they love her? Who knew? But she loved them. She'd always loved them because they were the angels she'd been dreaming would rescue her since she was old enough to understand what her virginity was.

"She feels so good, oh." Blond squeezed her head, his shaft thickening against all corners of her mouth. "I'm right on the edge, my pet. I'm gonna come." He came and didn't shield her, but emptied his entire seed into her mouth and held her head there until she drank every drop. "Ooh. Oh, God." He trembled afterwards as if it were 30 below zero weather. "That was amazing." He rubbed his dirty thumb across her damp lips.

"Mm." Black Hair didn't miss one beat, licking her clit with deliberate urgency.

"Oh." Clara's knees collapsed, and she fell to the dirt, squirming and bucking as she neared the magical edge. "Yes! Oh, God. Don't stop." She rubbed her titty through her chemise and wondered why the hell she still had it on. "I... ooh..." Clara erupted right inside his mouth, squirting with full force. She felt a little guilty seeing how he'd been more considerate, but she'd let Black Hair get his revenge if he needed to. "I'm sorry." She panted. "I couldn't help myself."

He moaned with pleasure and she turned to see him desperately licking her love juice from his mouth and chin. "You're delicious. Like fine wine. I need more of it."

"Me too," Blond said. "Sit regular and spread your legs wide."

"Your wish is my command, sir." Clara pulled her chemise completely off this time and spread her legs as wide as she could.

The men got in between them, side-by-side, equally licking and kissing in between her thighs.

"Oh." Clara massaged her burning nipples, not knowing how she wouldn't split in two because it felt so good.

They took turns sucking her clit. Blond would take a few lashes and then Black Hair. On and on and on, while Clara squealed for mercy that she hoped they didn't give. All the while, their masks stayed intact even though she was dying to see them, but the masks made the moment so erotic.

"We're gonna drink you dry, pet," Blond lowered his head and stuck his tongue inside of her while Black Hair kept licking her clit.

"Oh, my loves." She wrapped her legs around them. "This is better than my dreams! I never knew it could feel this good."

They licked and sucked as she felt another tidal wave bubbling inside her gut. Then, squeezing them both in her thighs, she came again, flooding Blond's face while Black Hair kept licking.

"Mm." Clara closed her eyes, grabbing Black Hair's head. "I'm coming again. Now... now. Oh!"

Again! Yes, again she came. A virgin. Three times in a row. She didn't know if this was normal, but she could surely get used to it.

She just held them there for a few minutes, stroking Black Hair's silky head and Blond's soft curls. A true bonding moment. She knew then she'd never be closer to any man like she was her delicious robbers. Or heroes. Whatever.

The men rose, each taking a nipple into their mouths. Once again, playing naughty tag team games that had her begging for more.

"I love you both." She felt silly saying it, but it was how she felt. She didn't want this to end.

Didn't wanna go back to her old life. Then she remembered, she didn't know their intentions. Maybe they'd kill her. But being with them felt so good she didn't care.

Smirking, Black Hair stood and pulled her up. "Are you tired?"

She shook her head. "I could never be tired of either of you."

Blond rose behind her, kissing up her back along the way. "You're the most beautiful woman I've ever seen."

Black Hair stood in front of her while Blond stood in the back.

Her chest felt tight again, her stomach twisting into knots. They were about to enter her at the same time! She'd never dreamed.

Black Hair lifted her leg and as he kissed her, slipped his cock inside of her and rocked gently, slowly.

"Sh." Blond didn't just ram inside of her rear. He kissed and massaged it a bit, getting her even wetter, and as she held her breath, he inched inside her rectum. He couldn't do it fast because she was way too tight and though he was stretching her to where she wanted to scream for him to stop, she wouldn't dare. Even the pain was worth sharing this moment with her first loves.

With her arms wrapped firmly around Black Hair, Clara rocked to the soothing music their bodies made together.

This was passion. This was love. It was all she waited for and she could feel with each stroke and how they shared her body so tenderly that they felt the same way.

"This doesn't... have to end." Black Hair grunted. "I've never felt this connected to anyone before."

"Me too." Blond moaned in Clara's ear, thrusting gingerly. "From this one afternoon, I see you're the woman I want in my life forever."

"I love you both, too." Consumed with being loved deeper than anyone could fathom, Clara took turns kissing the men, letting her lips linger longer than needed. "But I need to see you." She stroked Black Hair's mask. "Both of you."

"I want you to, my love." Black Hair's face distorted into a deep scowl as she felt him nearing orgasm. "Oh... lift my mask."

Clara hesitated. She wanted to see their faces but was afraid that after the mystery was gone,

she wouldn't feel the same. Holding her breath and trusting her heart, she slipped his mask off his

face.

He was a beautiful man. Not just because of his dominant, masculine features and sparkling eyes. But because she could see his emotions now. She'd felt him and he'd told her, but now she saw them. She'd never doubt his heart from this moment on.

"And me, darling." Blond gyrated inside her, widening her tender butthole. "Lift my mask."

While both men thrusted, stretching her to glory, Clara turned and snatched off Blond's mask. Like Black Hair, he shined with a beauty indescribable.

Clara turned her head left and right, giving them an equal opportunity to enjoy her tongue. "Please don't take me back." She held Black Hair's shoulder while holding onto Blond's head from behind. "You've given me everything I've dreamed of and I want more. I've waited for both of you all my life."

Black Hair smiled.

"I didn't know when or how you'd come, but I waited." She kissed them both again. "I never gave up on love."

"You're a part of us now," Blond said. "Continue with us on our journey and we'll give you anything you could ever want."

Any decent woman would've said no to gallivanting off with two criminals. But then again, a decent woman wouldn't be standing in the Montana mountains while one man fucked her from the front and the other from the back at the same time.

Clara giggled as she laid her head on Black Hair's chest, feeling his heart beat as both men made love to her.

Why would she ever want to be decent, anyway?

When decent is so boring?

THE END

SAMPLE OF SEX IN KENYA BELOW:

CHAPTER ONE

(2018)

"Will you stop bitching every five minutes?" Adam Jessup scrolled through his phone while he and Vette Marlon waited at the baggage carousel for their luggage. "Since we left the US, you've been complaining about everything."

"I'm hot." She fanned her face with a pamphlet, her curly yellow hair stuffed underneath her straw hat. "It's like four hundred degrees in this place. God. And why is everyone staring at us? Because we're white?"

Adam exhaled, checking the hotel reservations on his phone. "Maybe because you're being a bitch."

"Excuse me?" She moved aside as people grabbed their luggage. "You're the one with an attitude the whole time."

"That's because you complain about every damn thing." Adam stuffed his phone in his pocket. "Of course it's hot. It's Africa!"

Since he'd been a child, 30-year-old Adam's mother always told him that good people got their wish. So after all these years of living a squeaky-clean life, being an upstanding citizen and going to church even when his friends made fun of him for missing all the Sunday games, he'd finally made it to Africa.

The Global Health Foundation had sent him to Nairobi, Kenya to oversee a shipment of supplies to a local food bank. After six years of volunteering with the GHF, they'd tasked him with his first unsupervised mission and it made him damn proud.

Too bad he'd come with loud ass Vette Marlon who'd complained since they gotten off the plane. It would take a hell of a lot for Adam to hold his tongue on this trip.

They grabbed their bags from the carousel.

"This is for charity." Adam huffed as they walked toward the glass doors with people sliding in and out of them. "Think about the reason we're here."

"I don't wanna be here." Vette hurried alongside him in flip-flops. "I hate this place already. It's so hot I can't even see. Look at me, Adam." She threw out her white arm, the color of a snowstorm. "I'm paler than the average white person. I'm fuckin' translucent. You know what this sun will do to my skin? I got on five bottles of sunblock and that ain't even helping."

People gaped at Vette as she and Adam passed.

"Everyone's looking at you," Adam said. "Stop acting like a moron."

"So I'm making this up?" Her sandals clacked against the tile.

"It's not

hot to you?"

"We're from Florida, remember?" Adam huffed as they exited the airport. "You should be used to the heat... God damn." The sun punched Adam in the face as soon as they got outside. "Jesus." He slipped on his shades.

"Uh-huh." Vette folded her arms, thin mouth in a permanent scowl. "So who's complaining now?"

"Shit, my cap's in my damn luggage."

Vette grinned. "Want my hat? Sike."

"Whatever." He wiggled his toes in his Nikes. "I got on sneakers and thick socks and the sun is still burning my feet. And you got on flip-flops?" Adam looked around, noticing they seemed to be the only ones sweating and complaining. "The cement's burning through my shoes. I ain't never experienced heat like this."

"Please, *please*." Vette squeezed her hands together. "Tell me it isn't too late to go back."

"Let's find a cab, get to the hotel and out of this heat."

She saluted him. "Aye, aye, Captain!"

He mumbled, rolling his eyes.

CHAPTER TWO

If Adam expected Vette to chill once they got into the air-conditioned cab, he was wrong. She complained about the smell of the cab and that there wasn't enough room in the back to stretch her legs. But Adam refused to let these inconveniences bother him. No. He kept his mind on the sights. He tried to guess how many people there were in this little block alone, but there had to be hundreds. People walking on top of each other, in the middle of the street, through traffic. A car meant shit to them.

Brown and black ashy feet in dusty sandals. People yelling and cars honking. Bumper-to-bumper traffic. Long, ragged streets. Hustlers in old T-shirts and faded jeans looking to score off dumb tourists.

"Look at 'em." Vette took off her hat, looking around with narrow, cynical green eyes. "Like roaches."

"Shut up." Adam nudged Vette with his elbow.

The driver peeked at her from the corner of his eye.

"For some reason you thought you being in charge of this trip meant you're in charge of *me*." Vette nudged Adam back. "Well, you're not. Yeah, I said it," she yelled for the driver to hear. "They're like roaches. Walking all on top of each other. All in the streets like they don't know how to act. This isn't acceptable where we come from—"

"*Watch* it." Adam grabbed her wrist. "You don't want to sound racist do you, Vette?"

She rolled her eyes.

It wasn't that Adam was surprised. Everyone knew Vette was a racist bitch, but Adam had hoped she'd have *some* decorum for the sake of decency.

"Hey it's okay." The bright-eyed, purple-skinned driver snickered, rolling a toothpick in his mouth. "Let the lady talk. It don't bother me. She's showing her ignorance."

"Ignorance?" The imprint of Vette's bouncing breasts showed through her sweaty T-shirt. "Ain't that the pot calling the kettle black? And I mean *blacker* than *black*."

"Shut the fuck up!" Adam grabbed her arm. "I'm warning you."

"Get off me!" She struggled to free herself. "Who do you think you are?"

"I'm sorry, sir," Adam told the driver. "Believe me, I wouldn't have brought her if I didn't have to."

Vette scoffed. "No I was the only one who would come with you to this place. Let go of me, Adam." She hit him and he turned her loose.

"Is she drunk?" the driver asked.

Adam plopped back in the seat. "It's the one time she needs to be."

"A drink." Vette's eyes lit up. "That's what I need." She dug in her

purse and pulled out a tiny bottle of vodka.

Adam grabbed it before she took a swig. "What the fuck are you doing? I said no alcohol on this trip, Vette."

"Excuse me." She snatched the bottle back, batting her long lashes. "Are you my daddy? I'm twenty-eight-years-old. I can drink whenever I fucking want to."

He took the bottle again. "I'm not gonna have you sloppy drunk and acting like a fool on this trip. No drinking." He stuffed the bottle in his pocket. "You settle down."

She crossed her arms, smacking her lips.

"We're gonna go to the hotel, refresh, get to the food bank and help with the shipment. Drop the attitude, Vette. I'm warning you."

"Eat me, Adam." She squinted. "Oh, I forgot. You already did."

The driver chuckled.

Adam groaned. "Bitch."

****

"Thank God we're here!" Vette plopped down on Adam's hotel bed.

"I'm glad we got rooms right next to each other. Ah." She kicked off her

shoes. "I'm drained. That flight took everything out of me."

Whenever the GHF sent volunteers on overseas assignments, they always paid for the rooms and while Adam had been stuck in some dumps before, the Foundation didn't do too shabby this time.

A multi-room suite wrapped in subtle, yellow lighting brought charm to the dreary brown walls. Sand-colored curtains made the space cozier while the chic furniture stayed true to the room's swanky integrity.

"This is pretty nice, huh?" Adam opened the intricate wooden doors of the balcony, greeted by the sticky humidity.

"Are you crazy?" Vette scoffed. "I'm dying to get out of the heat and you're going back into it?"

Adam rested on the aluminum railing, admiring the city across the horizon. "You can see everything from here. Wow, look at that pool. It's huge."

"I'll pass."

"Come on, Vette. Compared to the places the GHF has put us in, you gotta admit this is beautiful."

"It should be with all the work we do for them and for *free,* I might add."

Adam expected to find a hotel like this in ritzy Florida spots like Boca Grande or Naples, not tucked away in a quiet corner away from the rest of Nairobi.

"Did you see how the guy at the front desk was looking at us?" Vette asked.

Adam chuckled. "Everyone's been looking at us."

"Yeah, well." Vette stood, rubbing the bedspread. "I don't like it. Make sure you lock up your stuff. They'll come in our rooms and rob us blind."

"Why?" Adam scratched his arm. "Neither of us have shit. We're broker than two jokes."

"You know how they are."

He looked back at her. "Do me a favor? While we're here, keep your racist comments to yourself because I don't appreciate them."

"Racist? Come on, you've heard how they are here in Africa."

"How are *they*?"

"Please. You can be Mr. Woke all you want to, but it's just us now. Why do you think everyone warned us about the crime in this place? They didn't just make it up."

"And there's not crime in Florida?"

"Yes, there's definitely crime in Florida and look who's committing it." She stretched. "I was born in Tallahassee, and I barely recognize it now. Every sign's in Mexican. The neiGHForhoods are a mess. It wasn't like that before—"

"I don't wanna hear this shit."

"Look at California. The Mexicans took over, and it's a dump."

"Why are you even a part of the GHF with the way you are? You do realize many who need our help are not white?"

"Don't give me that. You know how they all are."

"*Who*?" he shouted.

"The blacks, the Mexicans, Muslims, name them."

"Get the fuck out of my room."

"I'm not trying to fight with you—"

"Go!" He pointed at the door. "Don't make me throw you out."

"Fine." She snatched her purse, swung it over her shoulder and twisted to the door. "I'll be in my room if you need me."

Adam rolled his eyes as he turned back to the balcony. "I won't."

"You won't? Are you sure about that?"

"More than sure, Vette." He kept his back to her, enraptured by the aroma of fruit and spices from the street markets.

"Hmm." She joined him on the balcony and stood right behind him. "You're lying." She walked her delicate fingers down his sweaty nape. "Remember our night, Adam? After the GHF Christmas party last year?"

He sighed, flinching at her touch.

"We had a moment, wouldn't you say?" She hugged him from behind. "I bet you hadn't felt that good in a long time. Remember, how upset you were that night because your wife left you? I was there, Adam." She lay against his back, squeezing his abs. "I was there when you had no one else."

CHAPTER THREE

"Vette." Adam pulled at her hands. "Leave."

"Why are you treating me this way?" she purred. "So mean and hateful with the things you say?"

"Oh, I'm not the one with the problem here." He pushed her away and faced her. "And let's not talk about who's mean and hateful."

"You enjoyed that night." She pushed curls out of her face. "You said you did."

"We were *drunk*. It was just one night when things got out of hand."

"*No*." She sucked her lip. "You wanted me. You can't deny the attraction." She tangled her fingers in his T-shirt. "Why would you want to?"

"I told you." He pushed her again. "It was a mistake. I don't have feelings for you, Vette."

"Yeah?" She lowered her stare to his crotch. "If I stayed in here long enough, you would."

"Out." He shoved her, causing her to stumble. "Go refresh or whatever so we can get to the food bank and do what they need us to do. That's why we came here, remember?"

"Fuck you." She sashayed off the balcony and grabbed her purse. "I got better things to do then hang around your stuck up ass all day."

"What?" He hurried into the room. "We're supposed to help the food bank—"

"You're so perfect and in charge, you do it."

"We have a job to do here. Why the fuck did you even sign up for this trip if you didn't want to help?"

"You're so smart, right?" She opened the door. "Guess." She left.

"Jesus." Adam shook off his frustration, because there were more important things to think about than Vette, and as he unpacked, someone knocked on his door.

"Mr. Adam?" a man beckoned with a high-pitched East African accent.

Adam recognized the voice of the front desk manager, Meshack, and answered the door. "Hello."

The giddy, yellow-skinned African with freckles dotting his face, grinned back from ear-to-ear. "Hello, Mr. Adam. I wanted to make sure you're settling in all right. Is the room sufficient for you?"

"Oh, yes it's lovely." Adam smiled, holding his waist. "Thank you. What can I do for you?"

"Well..." Meshack's sparse eyebrows danced. "It's more of what I can do for *you*." He held a lopsided grin as he raised on his tiptoes to peek over Adam's shoulder. "Is your uh, companion with you?"

"Companion?" Adam grimaced. "You mean Vette? No, she went to her room, I guess."

"Excuse me if I am prying, but are you not together?"

"Hell no." Adam shook his head. "No, no way."

"I can be of help to you then." The much-shorter man strutted inside, his name badge sitting crooked on his flabby chest. "I didn't want to share this in front of your lady friend, but we offer special 'amenities' for the gentlemen at the hotel if they're interested."

Adam squinted, closing the door. "Special amenities?"

"You know." Meshack leaned forward, eyebrow raised. "We like to make our guests' stay as pleasurable as possible."

"Ah." Adam snickered. "You're one of those hotels that hire out prostitutes for tourists?"

"Not prostitutes. *Escorts*. It goes beyond sex. She will show you around the city and spend time with you. We deal with a company and everything is safe and reputable." Meshack told Adam the name of the company. "The women are gorgeous, clean and STD-free."

Adam scratched the back of his head. "That's not really my thing—"

"Sometimes you don't know what your thing is until you try it." Meshack winked. "This is a professional service, the women are of age, they get paid fairly and are treated very well." He twisted his face. "No trafficking, drugs or abuse, no. I'd never condone anything like that. You just get the company of a beautiful woman to help you pass the time." He smiled. "Surely, you can't say no to *that*."

CHAPTER FOUR

Adam checked in with the food bank and got back to the hotel by nightfall. He stopped at Vette's room, but she didn't answer. Either she'd left or was ignoring him and though he regretted throwing her out of his room earlier, he was too exhausted for her bullshit.

Drained, Adam headed to bed when someone knocked on his door around 9 PM. He greeted a stunning African woman with a purse on her arm and a large basketful of towels, soaps, and lotions.

The escort.

Shit. He'd forgotten about her.

She smiled with the whitest teeth he'd ever seen. Cinnamon-brown eyes sparkled against her rich, chestnut-brown skin.

She slipped inside the room smelling of coconut.

Adam was 6'2 so according to where her head hit him she was at least 5'9. God had blessed her with elegant, narrow features that enthralled a man on the spot.

She sashayed to the dresser, the multicolored wrap dress massaging her sleek, thin frame. She turned and smiled at Adam. "Hujambo," which meant, "hello" in Swahili. "My name is Grace Gitau. It's nice to meet you, Mr. Jessup. I hope you are enjoying your stay in Nairobi so far."

Grace?

Adam expected some exotic African name. "Thank you." He cleared his

throat. "Nairobi's lovelier than I could imagine."

And so are you.

"This might sound stupid." He chuckled. "But I'm guessing you're the escort?"

Her tiny, triangular-shaped breasts jiggled underneath the sheer material. "Yes."

"Okay." He exhaled, rocking. "I've never done this before."

"I understand."

His loins melted at the sound of her sultry accent. "Forgive me if I'm a little nervous."

"You've been with ladies before, haven't you?"

"Of course."

She blinked. "This is no different."

"I disagree." Adam chuckled, rubbing his hair. "I've never been with a complete stranger."

"That's what makes this easier." She wiggled her shoulders. Everything she did spelled sex.

"Emotions get in the way." She smiled. "Sometimes it's best to let your mind rest and have your body take control."

He nodded. "Guess I never thought of it as so straightforward."

"It can be." Grace took off her head wrap showing him her braids in a pristine bun and then her phone rang, destroying the intimacy. "Excuse me." She rushed to the dresser and grimaced as she got her cell out of her purse. "It is nothing." She sighed. "Sorry about that."

"Everything's okay?"

"Yes." She fidgeted as she put her phone away. "What were we talking about?"

"About this uh... arrangement." Adam chuckled. "It's new to me and all."

Her phone rang again.

She huffed as she yanked the phone out again. "I apologize."

"No, it's no problem. If you need to take that I can wait—"

"No." She stabbed her finger into the phone. "I will turn it on vibrate."

"You sure everything is okay?"

"Just an overzealous client." She flashed a forced smile as she sat on the bed. "Just ignore it if it buzzes. You're enjoying the city?"

"Yes."

"What do you like about it so far?"

"Well…" Sweat beaded on the back of Adam's neck, but it wasn't from the heat. "I haven't seen any sights yet, but I like the hotel and the food is amazing. Meshack said you can show me around the city?"

"I'd love to." She looked up at him through her flirty lashes. "I'm here to make your trip as pleasurable as possible. You've paid for a good time and I plan to give it to you."

Like any other business deal, Grace showed him her ID, proving her age of twenty-eight and even presented a document showing she was healthy and free of any disease. She spelled out the rules. No kissing on the lips, no weird or outrageous sex acts, and no action without use protection. If he didn't agree, no deal.

"I'm confused," Adam said. "Why does the company not allow kisses?"

"It's not *them*, Mr. Jessup." She put the document back into her purse. "The kissing is *my* rule. I don't allow my clients to kiss me on the lips."

"Why not?"

"Because kissing is too personal."

"Hold on." He laughed. "You can have intercourse with random men but they can't kiss you?"

"These are the rules." She shrugged one shoulder. "If you don't agree I will leave."

"No, it's just I don't see why kissing is different from everything else."

"It's just a line I won't cross."

"What if I forget? I mean, when we're into it? What if I do it by accident?"

"You won't."

"How do you know?"

Her mouth rose in the corner as she smiled. "I'll remind you."

He didn't like this. Didn't like it at all. Adam loved kissing. It was his favorite part of having sex.

Shit, he paid for her, he should be able to kiss her if he wanted.

He'd accept it because the last thing he wanted was Grace leaving. And though he didn't like this no-kissing shit one bit, he would savor every moment with this African goddess. Kiss or not, she'd been the woman of his dreams before he knew she existed.

CHAPTER FIVE

Grace removed her dress and glided to Adam buck-naked with no qualms at all and unbuttoned his shirt. His heart flip-flopped like it did when that sexy doctor gave him that penis exam a few years back when he had that savage urinary tract infection.

Grace moved like a robot, undressing him without batting an eye. Her mind trained on the mission. She was the escort, but Adam worried about pleasing *her*. He was no nervous he couldn't imagine getting into his groove. What if he were so bad she canceled the arrangement and gave him a refund? Talk about embarrassing.

"Relax." She smiled.

"Have you ever been with a woman?" he blurted out, not knowing why the hell he had.

She wiggled her dainty nose. "No."

"Did I offend you?"

She laughed. "Why would I be offended?" She threw his shirt on the floor. "You'd be shocked what clients ask me." She bent down, yanking at his zipper.

"*Whoa.*" He jerked, chuckling. "You don't waste time, do you?"

Her stiff, black nipples jiggled as she removed his pants.

"You said you get a lot of weird questions from clients?"

"It comes with the territory." She stood upright. "Some think that because I'm an escort, I have no boundaries. You won't believe what some people want me to do." She held her waist, perky breasts standing at attention. "There's some very freaky people out here."

Adam clenched his dick through his underwear, imagining how her mouth would feel on it. "Anyone ever get rough with you?"

"Some have tried, but I can handle myself."

He stared at her nipples, looking like giant Hershey's Kisses.

"Sit down," she commanded.

Adam sat, and she bent down in front of him, snatching off his socks.

Here he was sitting in front of her with this big, swollen pink cock ajar in her face and she looked at it like a secretary filing papers. Of course this was a job to her, but Adam expected a smile, a moan, any acknowledgement of his blessed member. After all, this cock had sent his soon-to-be ex-wife into fits of infinite ecstasy, but Grace's aloof reaction made him wonder just how many men she'd fucked.

She fluttered her long lashes. "We're going to take a shower."

"Huh?"

"Come on." She grabbed the basket and went to the bathroom.

By the time Adam got in there she was already under the water, standing against the tile wall, staring at him. "Get in."

He swallowed, even the creases in the bend of his knees sweated.

Oh, make no mistake. He wanted to fuck her. Wanted to beat the brakes off that sweet, African punani but paying for it just felt desperate and awkward. And it didn't help that Grace looked at his dick like a scientist in a laboratory.

"You ever had sex in the shower?" she asked.

"I've had sex in lots of places."

"Ah." She raised an eyebrow. "Get a lot of women?"

"Can't complain."

He wasn't cocky but he'd never met a woman who didn't find him

attractive. So he'd never had a problem finding fuck partners and though he'd been faithful to his wife, he'd been surprised at how many women didn't give a damn he was married and tried to get a spin on his old "love rod" anyway.

Grace tilted her head. "You're a ladies man?"

"I wouldn't say *that*. I mean I don't do nothing for it to happen. Women just like me."

She grinned. "I see."

"I'm not trying to be arrogant." He chuckled, waving off his last statement. "But it's true. Just something about me I guess."

"There definitely is." Grace's stare showered his body. "You are a beautiful man, Adam. Coal-black hair and killer blue eyes. Great body."

He tingled, clearing his throat. "Thank you." He stepped under the water and grinned as the warm sprinkles tickled his nipples.

"I bet your father is so handsome," Grace said.

"I wouldn't know."

She gaped.

"Never met the man or seen one picture." He scratched his arm. "Apparently he was just some dude my mom banged after meeting him in a bar."

"I'm sorry."

"It's okay. You don't miss what you never had."

"You don't know anything about him?"

"Mom stayed tightlipped but I have heard rumors through the years that he was married when they hooked up. Either way he doesn't want nothing to do with me."

She stuck out her chin. "How do *you* know?"

"I figure if he wanted to know me he'd been around."

"But you don't know if he tried to be around you. You have no idea what happened between him and your mother. Maybe he wanted to be in your life but your mother didn't want him to be."

He shook his head. "No, no."

"How do you *know*, Adam?" She clasped his wrist. "If your mother never said the reason and you've never met the man, you're just guessing." She let him go. "Don't judge your father when you can't be sure of what's going on."

"You're right. I don't know but still, if any woman tried to keep me from my kid, I'd do all I could to see him. So that's why I think he's full of shit. Sorry I just do. Can we talk about something else?"

"Like your penis?" She chuckled as she reached out the shower and got a rag from the basket. "I like it." Grace flung him around and washed his back and shoulders.

As if he wasn't nervous enough, he got an intense cramp in the pit of his stomach and cursed himself for having that steak and onions for dinner.

Shit. Please don't fart.

He held it in until the pain subsided and his ass relaxed.

Thank God.

If he'd farted, he might've blown poor Grace back into the hallway.

"You're so tense." She kneeled while working the rag up his thighs, the aromatic soap scenting the bathroom.

She washed between his wet cheeks, massaging his asshole, his dick about to pop.

"Mm." He grabbed it with both hands.

She snickered. "Feel good?"

"Yeah." He wiggled his toes in the water. "You need to bathe me more often."

She smiled. "There you go. You're relaxing. Hold on because the fun's just beginning. Turn around."

He did, and she washed his abdomen, dragging the rag through his thick, black pubic hair.

He glared down at her, talking to her with his eyes.

Get the tip. Please, please get the tip.

She finished washing or *teasing* him and smiled. "Your turn."

"Uh, okay." Adam got a new rag out the basket.

Grace turned around and pressed her hands to the wet tile, tight little brown ass shining with water. "Take your time."

Adam glided the rag over her glossy skin, exploring every inch of her.

The shifting muscles in her back. The curve of her bony hips, the smooth, never-ending length of her creamy legs.

"How did you get into escorting?"

She glanced at him over her skinny shoulder. "Kind of personal, you think?"

"We're two strangers sharing a shower." He grinned as he turned her around, looking right into her delicious nipples. "I think we're passed subtleties."

"Just circumstances, I guess." She pursed her pouty lips, creases running through her forehead. "There aren't many options around here especially for women. You do what you need to, to survive."

"I don't buy that." He massaged her arm with the rag. "You seem like a resourceful woman. There's gotta be more you can do than this."

She raised her eyebrows. "Are you saying you have an issue with my line of work?"

"I can't complain about any occupation that puts a beautiful woman in my shower unless you're not being treated right. I hope that's not the case."

"The company I work for? Oh, no it's wonderful. Very professional place. I'm not forced to do anything I don't want. It's just like any other job. We sign contracts and are held to high standards and we even get bonuses."

"Bonuses, huh?" He pinched her cheek. "What do you have to do for these bonuses?"

She wriggled, coyly. "I'm not being abused and I can walk away at any time. I choose to do this because compared to anything else, it's one of the best ways I can make money fast to help my family. Besides, if I wasn't an escort, we'd never met."

He smirked, squeezing out the rag.

"You're different. Clients usually don't care about my life. They just get what they want and go."

"Well, I'm not like that."

"Why are you here again?"

"In Kenya?" He licked his lips as he moved the rag over her kinky pussy hairs. "I'm a volunteer with the Global Health Foundation. They sent me to check the shipment for the food bank and help them get things organized."

"That's wonderful. How did you get into that?"

"Well, my mom always instilled in me how important it is to be a good person." He fondled her pussy through the rag. "That there is always someone out there that needs a hand, and I like helping people."

"I want to move to the States. I'm working toward my Visa."

"That's great."

"Where are you from?"

"Tallahassee, Florida."

"Really?" She gushed. "I have family in Miami."

"Wow, it is a small world, huh?"

"Do you travel a lot with the Foundation?"

"I've been all over the world, but it feels different this time."

"Why?"

"I don't know." His temperature rose as he looked into her soothing eyes. "Maybe it's the company."

She smiled and after he finished washing her, she went back to work on him, stroking and teasing.

Adam struggled not to climax, but Grace just wouldn't leave his cock alone.

"Ooh." He wobbled, holding the wall. "I'm coming."

"Yes, Adam." She rubbed faster, pointing his dick to her tits. "Come now. Give it to me. I want it so bad."

"Oh. Ah!" He ejaculated, squirting thick cream right on her chest. "Ooh. Fuck. "

Grace moaned, cum hanging from her nipples. "Good *boy*."

CHAPTER SIX

"Lay down," Grace ordered Adam once they got back into the bedroom. "Put your face into the pillow."

"What are we doing?"

"Trust me. You will like it."

Adam melted every time Grace touched him, and this time was no different. He breathed into the lavender-scented pillow as she massaged him, calming every muscle. His loins raced, dick swelling into another erection.

She climbed her damp, thin body onto his back and rubbed her furry pussy against the crease in his back.

"Hmm." Adam wiggled his toes, feeling as if he were floating on air. "This is *amazing*."

She leaned down, whispering into his ear. "It gets better."

He held his breath, nearly busting a nut on the sheet.

"Roll over."

He did, and she got on top of him again, massaging his chest while rolling her pussy against his cock.

"You like this?" She held a mischievous smile that told him she already knew he did.

"Fuck, yeah." He wiggled his erection against her. "Don't ever have to ask."

"It feels like..." She bounced, sending sharp sensations through his shaft. "You wanna fuck. Do you?"

"Again, you don't have to ask." He grinded against her moist labia but didn't enter. "I've wanted to fuck you since I saw you."

She blushed. "Do you like this position or something else?"

He loved that view of looking up at a woman's tits as she bounced on his dick, but he wanted to see that ass.

"Turn around." He narrowed his eyes. "Ride it from the other direction."

"Okay—"

"And take your hair down."

He loved pulling a woman's hair when he fucked her.

"Your wish is my command." She unwrapped her braids from the bun and flipped them over one shoulder.

"Yeah." He swallowed. "You are so beautiful."

She turned around, spread her ass cheeks apart with her hands and

sat on his dick.

"*Yes.*" Adam wrapped his hands into her braids. "That's it. Ride me, Grace."

"With pleasure—"

Her purse buzzed.

"Fuck." Adam groaned. "Your phone again."

"I...I apologize." She climbed off him and got her purse. "Sorry."

Adam sighed, scratching his balls.

"You've got to be kidding me." She read the screen. "Ten times?"

"What? Is that the same person from earlier?"

"I'm turning it off." She pressed her fingertip into the phone. "It's nothing."

"Doesn't seem like nothing. Is someone bothering you, Grace?"

"No, no." She got a condom from the basket and twisted back to the bed. "Please forget it."

"You keep walking like *that* and it'll be easy to. I love the way you walk."

She giggled, and it was the first time he noticed her dimples.

"Seriously," he said. "You can tell me if you need help."

"I'm fine, Adam. It's not your concern."

"You said it was a client earlier—"

"Please." She slipped the condom on him. "Don't ruin the mood."

"Okay." He took her hand. "Lay down."

"I thought you wanted me on top."

"Not anymore." He laid her down beside him and while stroking her braids, lost himself in her intoxicating eyes and attempted a kiss.

"No." She frowned, lifting her finger between their mouths.

Fuck it, he worked on her titty, sucking and flicking the nipple back and forth with his tongue. Sensing she was ready for him, he fondled her pussy and spread her sticky labia open.

Grace panted, catching her breath in her throat.

"Fuck foreplay." He rolled her over, mounted her and shoved his pulsating dick inside her.

She thrashed against him, grabbing at the sheets and moaning.

Her cunt made him feel like a starved, desperate dope feign who'd finally gotten his fix after stumbling around for days searching for a high. Every thrust introduced his dick to a unique sensation.

He thought his soon-to-be ex-wife Ronnie had been the best fuck he had, with drunk ass Vette a close second, but they didn't compare to Grace one bit.

"Right there, Grace." He squeezed his fingers into her soft flesh. "Oh."

Adam humped harder, the bed frame beating the wall like it was Floyd Mayweather. "Whose pussy is this, huh? Whose is it?"

"Yours."

"Who? Say my name." He yanked her braids. "Say my fucking name."

"It's yours, Adam!"

"You damn right it is." He moved faster, riding that cunt like a beast. "Say my name again. Loud!"

"Adam, yes!" She grabbed his arms, her titties bouncing from side-to-side. "Oh! Don't stop."

****

"No."

Adam awoke the next morning to Grace arguing in his bathroom. It took him a second to realize she was on the phone.

"I mean it," she said. "Leave me alone. I can't take this anymore."

Adam heard her heading out the bathroom and lay over, pretending he was still asleep. "Oh." He pretended to awake when she entered. "Hey there."

"Good morning, Adam." She glided to the bed in her dress, looking like a living portrait. "Did you sleep well?"

"The best sleep I've had in years." He stretched against the fluffy pillows. "You're dressed. Are you leaving? You promised to show me around the city today."

"I'd love to." Her white teeth gleamed. "And I shall. I have to run to my place to freshen up and then I'll be back." She gestured to her dress, grinning. "I don't want to go out in the same dress as last night."

"Why not?" He took her hand and pulled her on the bed. "You look gorgeous in it. You look even better out of it."

She set her cellphone on the nightstand.

"Let me guess. Was that the same person who called you all last night?"

"Sh." She pressed her finger to his lips.

"Mm." He put his arm around her waist. "Let me kiss you—"

"No." She jerked back. "No, Adam."

"In this moment, looking into my eyes and being this close, you're telling me you don't want to kiss me?" He inched his mouth to hers. "Come on—"

"Adam, I will leave." She pressed her lips together. "These are my rules. If you can't accept them—"

"Fine." He let her go, mumbling.

"Don't be mad." She stroked his cheek. "After this, you won't even think about a kiss." She got another condom and within moments, Grace had him hard as cement, riding his stick with animalistic fervor.

"Ah, yeah." Adam gripped her waist, bouncing her. "Yes, Grace." He pushed his back into the bed. "Yes."

The bed shrieked and squealed, shaking the nightstand off balance.

"I love your dick, Adam." She bounced harder. "You're so handsome."

He grunted. "Slow it down a bit. Ah."

If Grace's pussy had a name, it would've been "magic".

She spun her hips, gyrating and thrusting until he flooded the condom.

"Ahhhh." Adam jiggled her, draining every drop of cum into the rubber.

"Oh." She rolled over breathless, her brown body dotted in sweat. "You're so good."

He rubbed his sweaty abs. "Am I?"

"Oh, *yes*." She closed her eyes, her entire body trembling as she exhaled. "Many of my clients are horrible because they don't care about pleasing me and only getting off. But you please me, Adam."

"If you don't enjoy it then I won't." He kissed her hand. "I'm jealous."

"Jealous?"

"Of that client who keeps calling you. Guess he's hooked, huh? Can't blame him. I'm hooked now too."

"Adam." She leaned up. "You are getting confused."

"I'm not confused." He dragged his finger down her thigh. "I know exactly what I'm saying."

"I'm an escort, Adam." She swallowed. "This is just business."

"If you stay here long enough..." He held her neck, guiding her mouth to his. "It can be more—"

"No." She shook her head, pushing him away. "Please, stop, Adam."

"*Why*?" He let her go. "Why can you fuck me, bathe me, but I can't get a kiss?"

She avoided eye contact. "This is a job."

"Bullshit. How we talk, what we've shared, it's more than business."

"After one night?"

"Yes after one fuckin' night. I feel something for you, Grace. Already."

"I'll have sex with you anytime you want. Make your stay pleasurable, but we can't cross that line." She tightened her lips. "No kissing."

"Fuck that." Adam grabbed her again. He never manhandled women, but he needed to kiss her if only to make her realize this was more than a job. Or maybe convince himself it was. "Come here." He grabbed her skinny face.

"No!" She fidgeted, whimpering and shoving. "Stop it."

He let her go and slammed his head against the pillow.

"You want me to leave and not come back? Because you're acting like an animal."

He sighed into his hands.

"You say you're different than my other clients but you're acting just like them." She stood. "Like just because you pay for my time you own me. Well, you do not." She twisted to the dresser and got her ponytail holder. "I will not be disrespected."

"Fuck, Grace, I'm human. I *want* to kiss you. I'm not apologizing for that."

"What is it with you men? What women say isn't important?"

"I didn't say that."

"I don't belong to you or any man." She wrapped the ponytail holder around her hair and twisted her braids into a bun. "I am tired of men thinking they can take anything they want from me. Tired, Adam."

"All right calm down. Jeez." He straightened the pillow behind his head. "I won't do it again."

"You better not." She got her phone from the nightstand. "Or money or not, this is over."

CHAPTER SEVEN

"Hello, Grace." Sokoro Otieno greeted her when she entered her home, his voice so deep it shook the octagon tiles of her living room.

"What is this?" She yanked her key out her door before closing it. "Sokoro, what are you doing in my house?"

The 32-year-old lothario remained on her white sectional, his 6'5 body tucked into jeans and a white Gucci blazer, gold jewelry glistening from his silky, cocoa-brown skin. "I'm tired of you ignoring me."

She threw her purse on the glass coffee table. "Get out of my house or I'll call the law."

"The law?" He laughed, his perfect square teeth so white they could light up the darkness. "You forget who I am, Grace? I own the law. Everyone around here does what I say and you will be no different."

"Why are you doing this? Please, leave me alone."

"You weren't telling me to leave you alone after I gave your family that one million shillings when the white man tried to force your family off their land, were you?" He rubbed his slick, bald head, angular cheeks flexing with every word he spoke. "Weren't telling me to go away when your family needed money for food or when your mother got sick and couldn't afford her medication. What's changed?"

"We didn't know we'd made a deal with the devil."

"You should've known." He lifted his athletic frame off the couch, closing his blazer. "You refuse me, Grace? I'm royalty around here. I got women throwing themselves at my feet—"

"Then harass *them*. I won't nothing to do with you, Sokoro. Leave me and my family alone or you will be sorry."

His cackle rattled through her, shaking the walls. "Oh, that's what I love about you, Grace. Your spunk. Not that your beauty isn't more than enough to keep a man satisfied and your uh..." He walked his stare down her body. "Your other attributes. Should I mention them?"

"You'll never have me, Sokoro."

"Is that, right? Oh, wait. I had you already." He winked. "More than once. Did you forget?"

"You had my body." She stuck her chin in the air. "Not my heart. That you'll never get no matter how much money you have or how many times you threaten my family."

"I wouldn't be so sure." He straightened his sleeve. "Either your family pays the debt they owe for me saving that godforsaken dump of a village, or you marry me." His wide smile took up his entire face. "Simple as that."

"Never!"

"Come on, Grace. Let me make an honest woman out of you. You can't like slinging your body to every tourist that comes into town."

"I'd rather fuck every scoundrel on this earth than to be with you. You don't even need the money, Sokoro. You do this to torture us. To show you're in control."

"So because I'm well off, I don't deserve my money back?" He shook his head, clicking his jaw. "What world are you living in, Grace? You expect thousands for free and me get nothing? I'm not even asking for all the other times your sniveling joke of a father came begging me for money."

"Stop it." She got on her tiptoes but didn't reach anywhere close to his face. "My father is an honorable man. Ten times the man you'll ever be."

"So honorable he can't even support his family? Living in that pigsty village? Is that what you want to go back to, Grace?" He frowned. "The bush? Bathing with the same animals you eat? Drinking their feces? You want to live like an animal?"

"Don't you ever talk about my family that way. We are proud people!"

"So proud that your parents pimp their daughter out for money?"

She raised her hand to slap him, but he grabbed it.

"Uh-uh." He squinted his espresso-brown eyes. "You'd better think about that real quick, Sweetheart. Let's not get violent, Grace. You won't win that fight."

"Let me go!" She snatched her hand free.

"Marry me."

"You don't have to force a woman into marriage." She rubbed her aching wrist. "You're gorgeous and rich. You could have any woman you want."

"And I want *you*. Why is that so hard for you to understand?"

She rocked. "I'll get you the money myself."

He laughed. "You gonna suck every dick in Nairobi? Because that's what it will take for you to raise what your family owes me. You're doing well for yourself Grace, but not *that* well." He walked around her living room of slate-blue walls and icy-gray tile floor. "This is a beautiful home, but we know it wasn't easy for the village girl to come up. How do you think you rented this place, Grace?"

"With the money I make." She grimaced. "How the fuck do you think?"

"You have no credit." He walked behind the couch, massaging the back of it as he did. "Even with what you make, how do you think you got a deal on a place like this in this neiGHForhood?"

She held her breath.

"Me, Grace." He walked across the rug to the connecting kitchen. "I got this place for you."

"Liar! I bought this with *my* money."

"Because I spoke to the owner."

She shook, gritting her teeth. "You're lying."

"Course he's no longer the owner." He got the carton of orange juice out of the refrigerator.

"What are you talking about?"

Sokoro stared at her as he drank. "Ah." He set the glass on the counter. "I own this house now. I bought it last week. Hello, Grace." He grinned. "Meet your new landlord."

"Filthy liar. You're lying to manipulate me."

"It is true." He walked out the kitchen, approaching her. "You can't get away from me, Grace. I own you just like I do this property. Now..." He caressed her shoulders as she fought not to vomit. "You can be a smart girl and realize all a life with me offers or you can go back to the bush and bathe with the rhinos. Of course, if your family doesn't repay me, your village will be gone and your family dead—"

"Sokoro." She covered her mouth, gasping. "Please leave my family alone. I beg you."

"Oh, Grace." He took off her head wrap and pushed his nose into her braids. "That's the deal. You do what I want or suffer the consequences."

"No." She punched his chest as he strangled her in his embrace. "I'll get you the money. Leave my family alone!"

"You'll get me the money?"

"Yes." She sobbed. "Yes!"

"Okay." He pulled her head back. "But I need some collateral." He unbuckled his belt with his free hand.

"No." She squeezed her eyes shut. "No, Sokoro."

"Sh." He lowered her on her knees as she trembled. "Be a good girl, Grace. Show your appreciation for all I've done."

"No, please." He held her head still as he unzipped his pants. "No!"

CHAPTER EIGHT

"Trust me, Adam." Grace accompanied Adam from his hotel room a few hours later. "I'll show you all Nairobi can offer."

"Sounds great but are you all right? You seem like something is on your mind."

"I'm fine." She smiled, yet Adam wasn't convinced. "We'll go everywhere. Let me see." Her eyes lit up as she clasped her hands, bracelets jiggling. "You like animals?"

"I love animals."

"Great. We'll go to the National Park and the Safari Walk."

"Sounds nice." He didn't care if they visited a dump as long as he could spend the day with Grace.

They walked downstairs. Grace's dress brushed the steps as her sandals held her delicate feet. "We'll go to the Karen Blixen Museum too. You'll love it!"

"Who is Karen Blixen?"

"*Adam.*" She groaned and even that sounded sexy. "Karen Blixen is the author of *Out of Africa.* Remember the movie with Meryl Streep and Robert Redford?"

"I remember the movie but didn't know it was a book." He laughed as they got to the first floor.

"The book is even better than the movie. It's the story of Karen's life in Africa." She stuck her skinny finger in the air. "You should read it. I'm a true romantic and that book blew me away."

"*You* blow me away."

Grace dipped her head, redness caressing her brown cheeks. "You are sweet."

"And you're amazing."

"Ah, Mr. Adam." Meshack rocked behind the front desk with a smile as wide as Canada. "Good day. Did you sleep well?"

"Very well." Adam stood at the counter, winking at Grace, who rolled her eyes with a snicker. "Everything's perfect."

"Well, I'm glad to hear that," Meshack said. "Grace is a sweetie and tourists love her. She knows the city well and will take care of you."

"I will." She batted her sweeping lashes.

Adam rubbed up against her. "And I want to be taken care *of*."

"Well, well, well," Vette walked down the stairs. "What do we have here?" She stopped in front of Grace and Adam with resting bitch face. "And you are?"

"I'm Grace." Grace bowed, holding her hand out to her. "It's nice to meet you."

Vette glared at her hand and then at Adam. "And where did he find you?"

Grace grimaced, pulling her hand back. "He didn't *find* me anywhere."

"Grace is a tour guide." Adam took Grace's arm. "I found her on the Internet. She's gonna show me around the city."

"Do I look stupid to you?" Vette crossed her arms. "If she's a tour guide than I'm your mother."

"Then we'll be seeing you, 'Mom.'" Adam rolled his eyes as he pulled Grace away toward the door. "We have things to do."

"So I'm not invited?" Vette scoffed.

"I invited you to see the sights yesterday. You didn't want to." Adam opened the door for Grace. "After you."

"You're just leaving me here?" Vette yelled. "What the fuck am I supposed to do?"

A passing woman gasped at the vulgarity.

"You're a resourceful woman, Vette." Adam winked. "I'm sure you'll find some way to entertain yourself." He helped Grace out the door.

"Who was that?" Grace asked as they exited the front steps.

"Nobody."

She faced him, fixing her purse on her shoulder. "She likes you."

He nodded, taking a stick of gum from his pocket. "How do you know?"

"I'm a woman." She patted his cheek. "We know *everything*."

CHAPTER NINE

Grace promised Adam a hell of a time and she did not disappoint. She showed Adam places he'd never heard of and the more Adam saw, the more curious he got. His heart warmed at every stop and he could feel why they called Africa "The Motherland". It wasn't just for black heritage, but Africa had lent so much of its beauty and authenticity to the American way of life that it was impossible for Adam not to be thankful.

After touring Ngong Hills, Grace took Adam to a two-story restaurant made of bamboo walls and decorated with East African artifacts. Striking waitresses strutted around in vibrant, multi-colored head wraps that matched their dresses.

Adam and Grace got an outside table where they could see the overlapping mountains in the distance.

Nairobi was unlike any place Adam had been because every experience was a part of its culture. The aroma of curry powder and strong native spices tickled his nose. The restaurant alone told Adam everything he needed to know about the city.

Grace ordered them beef curry along with her favorite and a very common Kenyan dish; Ugali, a porridge made of maize flour.

Food looked like a painting on the plates; bright, lively and rich with a variety of heat and spices which made Adam feel like he tasted African culture with each bite.

"You said this was super food." Adam chewed. "What makes it super?"

Grace sipped from her glass of apple juice with a straw. "Because it's my favorite."

He laughed. "That makes sense."

"Why? Do you not like it?"

"No, I love it. It's delicious. I love the spices. Don't tell my mom, but this is the best cooking I've ever had."

Grace smiled while chewing. "I grew up on this food."

"Are you a good cook?"

"Of course." She bounced, sitting back. "All Nairobi women can cook. It is a big part of our culture. Cooking is how we show love to our family. You should taste my cooking."

Adam rubbed the toe of his sneaker against her leg. "There's something else of yours I'd love to taste."

"I'm serious." She chuckled, swatting his foot away. "You should let me cook for you."

"I'd love that but might not have enough time."

"Oh." She dropped her stare to the table. "How long will you be in the city? I forgot to ask."

"A few more days."

Her face fell.

"Why?" His heart fluttered. "You hoping it will be more?"

She lifted her chin, shaking her shoulders. "No."

He didn't buy that one bit. She was starting to become attached to him as much as he had her.

The umbrellas above their heads, which shielded customers from the sun, shifted a bit in the muggy breeze.

Grace giggled, wincing.

"What?" Adam drank some of his tangy pineapple juice. "Why are you giggling?"

"It's you." She covered her mouth as she chewed. "You keep staring at me."

"Well, you're a beautiful woman."

"Stop." She laughed under her hand. "I don't want you watching me eat. Look at the mountains."

He turned his head away for a second then faced her again. "Nah, I'm good."

She snickered, wiping her mouth.

"You're amazing, Grace. You deserve the world."

"Many men have promised that to me." She waved her fork, swallowing. "But I don't want a man to give me anything, Adam."

"I doubt that." He sat back. "What about love? Don't you want *that*?"

"Romantic love is an illusion." She drew lines in her food with her fork. "At least for people like me."

"That's ridiculous. You telling me you've never been in love?"

"Where I come from, love is a luxury I can't afford. Other things take precedence. Like survival."

"So? Love has nothing to do with where we come from or what we've gone through. If love is coming, it's coming. We have no power over Cupid's arrow. If we did, we wouldn't let ourselves be so tortured by relationships or allow our hearts to be torn into shreds. People can't control love. It controls *you*. Plus, it always comes when you least expect it."

He caught the glimmer in her eye, which suggested she'd gotten the hint that he might've been talking about *them*.

"You've had a special love?" she asked. "One more important than the others?"

"Ronnie." He wiggled his mouth. "Veronica. My wife."

"Wife?" Grace gaped. "You're married?"

"Separated." He squeezed his cup. "About seven months."

"What happened?"

"She fell out of love with me." He shrugged, eyes watering. "Met a guy at her job who swept her off her feet and paid more attention to her than she felt I did."

"Is that true?"

"Guess so." His voice cracked from emotion. "I put all my time into the GHF, and I didn't realize Ronnie felt like she was just waiting on the sidelines. She thought I'd pull further away from the organization, but I got more into it. It put a huge strain on our marriage, me traveling all the time, but I love doing this and helping people."

Grace smiled.

"I love knowing I did something to make someone's life better."

She patted his hand. "I'm sorry, Adam. It's her loss."

"She loves someone else. It is what it is."

"Do you still love her?"

"I'll always love Ronnie. Once you're married, that person becomes a part of you. But we don't belong together and I accept that. I just want her to be happy. Besides, in all the time I've been with Ronnie, I've never felt like this."

Grace squeezed his hand. "To new beginnings, aye?"

"Exactly." Adam stared into her glowing eyes. "And I'm ready for them."

CHAPTER TEN

Adam followed Grace upstairs to his hotel room, enjoying every swivel of her body.

She turned from the door, blushing when she caught his stare. "I had a wonderful day, Adam. The most fun I've had in a long time."

"Don't you do this with all your clients?"

"Yes." She'd taken her head wrap off and was now playing with it in her hands. "But it never felt like this."

"Like what?" He leaned against the door, moving closer to her.

"I don't know." She dropped her head.

"You know." He lifted her chin. "You feel what I feel. Something you don't understand but you love it all the same."

"I'll come back tonight." She stepped back from the door. "Do you like to dance?"

"I like anything if I do it with you."

"There's a club I like to go to. It's not fancy, but I want to take you there. We'll have fun."

"I'd love that."

She turned to leave, and he put his arm around her waist. "I'm not done with you yet."

She tucked in her lips. "Is that so?"

He unlocked the door and pulled her over the threshold.

"What is this?"

He pushed her against the door. "This is me taking control." He kissed down her dress, pulling it up as he got on his knees.

She moaned, her head wrap slipping from her fingers.

Adam took off her white thong and sniffed the sweet, womanly scent of her bush, widening her legs until his tongue met her clit.

"Mm." Grace threw her leg over his shoulder, rocking as licked her labia. "Oh, Adam." She rubbed her tits, the end of her dress tickling his head. "Ooh."

He didn't lick hard, just tickled her clit with the tip of his tongue.

She gyrated, squeezing his head between her thighs.

He turned his head sideways, getting his tongue further inside her, his dick rising when he saw the pink walls of her vagina.

"Uh-huh." She ran her fingers through his hair. "Please don't stop, Adam."

He sucked until she released, drowning his tongue.

"Oh." Grace went limp, falling over as he held her. "Jesus."

He stood, swooped her into his arms and threw her on the bed face first.

"What are you gonna do?" she mumbled into the bedspread.

"You scared?" He panted, taking off his belt.

"No."

He bounded her wrists with his belt and pulled them over her head. "Don't move." He yanked up her dress, tearing the thin material on one side.

She gasped. "You tore it."

He grinned. "You won't care after this."

Adam kissed around her tight buttocks and spread them, sticking his tongue in her tight asshole.

"Oh, yes." She writhed. "Yes, Adam. My ass. Yes!"

He moaned as he sucked her anus, shocked even that part tasted good. Ass eating disgusted him before he met Ronnie. But after years of her begging him to rim her, he finally had and it had quickly become one of his favorite acts.

He'd thank Ronnie later.

"There!" Grace lifted her head. "Right there, Adam. Oh, I'm coming."

He spit on her ass and spread the moisture from her asshole all the way to her pussy. "God, I want you so bad." He pulled his zipper down so hard he almost tore it. "I'm gonna fuck you in the ass, Grace."

She writhed.

"Is that okay?"

"Yes but get a condom." She wiggled her hips. "Adam."

"I got this." He grabbed his pack of Magnums from his pants.

"Let me see it." She struggled to look over her shoulder and he realized she didn't trust him.

He showed it to her.

"Okay." She sighed, nodding.

"You don't trust me?"

"It's just that some men pretend to wear them and I can't tell."

"Grace." He caressed her side. "I'd never, ever do something so shitty."

She flashed a smile over her shoulder. "I know."

Not wanting the awkward conversation to kill the mood, Adam tore the condom open with his teeth, and slid it on his shaft. "You ready?"

"Yes, yes!" She pushed her face to the bed. "Fuck me, Adam."

He spread her cheeks so wide he could see her little hole pulsating. It had widened since he'd sucked it. To his surprise, it took a minimal amount of tugging and he was inside her. As he pumped, her ass clenched his shaft, squeezing every nerve.

"Yeah." He pulled her arms toward him, yanking the belt as he fucked her. "Ah." Her ass smothered his dick while wetness seeped from her pussy. "You're so wet, Grace. Ah."

"Yes." She bounced her head as he pounded her so hard their skin made slapping noises. "Ooh. Oh!"

Adam pumped, face drowning in sweat. "Grace. Oh!"

****

Grace laughed, laying naked beside Adam on the bed an hour later. "You always asking me so many questions."

He lay on his side on his elbow with his hand propped under his chin. "Tell me about your family and where you come from."

She played with her braids, which she'd swooped to one side. "I come from a village in Kibera, and I have seven brothers and a little sister."

Adam whistled. "Seven brothers? I better treat you right, huh?"

"Life is hard in Kibera, just poverty and grief. You'd be disgusted just seeing pictures of the place, but it is my home and where I learned to survive. Because of that, even with all the problems it has, I love it and I love my family."

He nodded.

"You can't imagine the things I've been through. Nothing was given

easily to me, Adam. I've worked for everything. Let me show you." She got her phone off the nightstand and Googled Kibera. "This is where I am from."

Adam took one look at the place and his heart bled. To Grace, this was home. To Adam, all he saw was sadness, desperation, and hardship.

Filthy shacks barely standing, using each other for balance. The stench of extreme poverty wafting from the images. A world built on trash, hopelessness and neglect. Neglect by a government that allowed its people to suffer in conditions not fit for a dog.

Adam scrolled through pictures and more and more his pity for the people turned into anger that anyone, even the United States could allow people in the world to live like this.

This was why. These pictures. These villages. This place. Is why Adam was a member of the GHF. He might not have the power to do a damn thing but he'd try. That was a promise.

"I'm gonna help you." He sniffed. "I'm gonna make sure the GHF helps in some kind of way because this isn't right, Grace. No one anywhere in the world should ever have to live like this."

She nodded.

"This isn't living." A tear skated down his cheek. "I don't mean to offend you. This is your home—"

"No." She caressed his arm. "It means the world to me that you care. I agree. This isn't a life for any human.

"I don't understand how people see this and don't care. Governments should protect their people. It's disgusting that you had to live like this. I can't..." He handed her the phone, closing his eyes. "I...I'm so sorry."

"I didn't mean to make you upset."

He wiped his eyes. "I hate seeing humans suffering like this. I don't know anyone with a heart that could look at those pictures and not cry. Not feel just the most sadness they've ever felt."

"You are a good man, Adam." She stroked his hair. "I wish there were more like you in the world but many do not care about others. That's what I saw the minute we met, your heart. It's what makes you who you are."

"In the States, we take so much for granted. In many countries, running water is a *luxury* when a basic right of any human should be access to clean water. It humbles you to see how others live."

"Before I moved to the city, I didn't even know what a toilet was." Grace laughed. "We used the resources God gave us and felt that was all we needed."

He kissed her arm. "I admire you for doing what you can to help your family."

She looked ahead. "I'm not proud of what I do, but it's the only choice I've had."

"Don't give up on your dreams, Grace. I know you want more."

"Course I want more. No one *wants* to sell themselves, but it's the hand that's been given to me. When I get to the States, I'm going to work in the medical field."

"A doctor?"

"A medical technician." She straightened her shoulders, pride bursting from her eyes. "My parents instilled in us the importance of education because without that you have nothing. They want me to have way more than they ever could."

Adam laid his head on the pillow. "I didn't go to college."

"You didn't?"

"No, I thought about it, but my mom couldn't afford it and I didn't want a bunch of student loans."

"What do you do?"

"I work for a lawn car service. I'm not raking it in, but it pays the bills. Barely." He chuckled.

"I don't want 'barely', Adam. I want 'success'. You have so much offered to you and you squander it away?"

"I didn't squander anything. Everyone doesn't have to go to college to be successful, Grace."

"Are you successful?" She gestured to him. "Do you want to do lawn service your whole life?"

"Well, no—"

"How about going to school so you can one day own the company you work for, Adam? Look at my circumstances. I refuse to let them stop me, then yours shouldn't stop you." She tapped his chest. "Go to school, Adam. Get student loans, whatever. Better yourself because you only get one chance."

"Wow." He scoffed.

"Did I offend you?"

"No." He pulled her into his arms. "You're amazing, Grace. Simply amazing."

Also by Stacy-Deanne

Billionaires For Black Girls
Billionaire for the Night
Billionaire Takes the Bride
Billionaire At 36k Feet
Billionaire's Love Trap
Billionaire in the Caribbean
Billionaire Broken
Billionaire Times Two

Sex in the Wild West Series
Maid for Two
Fling on the Frontier

Stripped Romantic Suspense Series
Stripped
Captured
Damaged
Haunted
Possessed
Destined

Stripped Series (Books 1-5)

Tate Valley Romantic Suspense Series
Now or Never
Now or Never
Chasing Forever
Chasing Forever
Sinner's Paradise
Sinner's Paradise
Last Dance
Last Dance

The Bruised Series
Bruised
Captivated
Disturbed
Entangled
Twisted

The Good Girls and Bad Boys Series
Who's That Girl?
You Know My Name
Hate the Game

The Studs of Clear Creek County
The White Knight Cowboy

The Forlorn Cowboy

Standalone
The Seventh District
Gonna Make You Mine
Empty
Gonna Make You Mine
Protecting Her Lover
What Grows in the Garden
Love is a Crime
On the Way to Heaven
Open Your Heart
Open Your Heart
A Matter of Time
Hero
Outside Woman
The Watchers
Harm a Fly
Harm a Fly
An Unexpected Love
You're the One
Worth the Risk
Hawaii Christmas Baby
The Best Christmas Ever
Prey
The Good Girls and Bad Boys Series
Bruised Complete Series
Tate Valley Complete Series
The Princess and the Thief
The Little Girl
The Stranger

Oleander

Seducing Her Father's Enemy

Love & Murder: 3-Book Romantic Suspense Starter Set

Paradise

Stalked by the Quarterback

Stripped Complete Series

Tell Me You Love Me

Five Days

Off the Grid

Sex in Kenya

Fatal Deception

A Cowboy's Debt

Billionaires for Black Girls Set (1-4)

A Savior for Christmas

The Samsville Setup

Trick The Treat

The Cowboy She Left in Wyoming

Theodore's Ring

Wrangle Me, Cowboy

The Billionaire's Slave

The Cowboy's Twin

Everwood County Plantation

Billionaires for Black Girls Set 5-7

The Lonely Hearts of San Sity

Stranded with Billionaire Grumpy Pants

Also by Venus Ray

Billionaires For Black Girls
Billionaire for the Night
Billionaire Takes the Bride
Billionaire At 36k Feet
Billionaire's Love Trap
Billionaire in the Caribbean
Billionaire Broken
Billionaire Times Two

Sex in the Wild West Series
Maid for Two
Fling on the Frontier

Standalone
Beast
Cindefella
Billionaires for Black Girls Set (1-4)

www.ingramcontent.com/pod-product-compliance
Lightning Source LLC
Chambersburg PA
CBHW061402160726
47995CB00001B/419